Disney
ELENA OF AVALOR

ELENA and NAOMI'S BIG ADVENTURE

Adapted by Silvia Olivas

Based on the episode "Finders Leapers," written by Silvia Olivas
for the series created by Craig Gerber

Illustrated by Studio Bosch and the Disney Storybook Art Team

Disney PRESS
Los Angeles • New York

SUSTAINABLE
FORESTRY
INITIATIVE
Certified Sourcing
www.sfiprogram.org
SFI-01415

igs the jaquin flies high over the city of Avalor with a bagful of his favorite snack—coconuts! Suddenly, Luna and Skylar zoom by and snatch the bag!

"Hey! Get your own lunch!" Migs shouts.

"We just did!" Skylar calls, chuckling.

But the bag is so heavy Skylar accidentally drops it! **BOOM!** The coconuts fall on a statue in the town square, which topples over and creates a huge hole in the ground!

The jaquins land and peer down into the hole to see a room filled with shiny gold objects!

"It's buried treasure!" Migs exclaims. "We'd better alert Princess Elena."

When Elena hears of the jaquins' discovery, she gathers the Grand Council. She asks Professor Mendoza to come, too. The professor is an expert on Maruvians, the people who lived in Avalor long ago.

"This is an ancient ruin!" Professor Mendoza proclaims. "It's filled with lost treasures!"

"I recommend a dig to remove anything valuable," says Chancellor Esteban. "Then we can repair the road."

Thinking the treasures could teach them about Avalor's history, Elena agrees. "Let's do it!"

Naomi offers to help with the dig. "I know a lot about Avalor's ruins," she says. "I used to play in them when I was younger."

Elena thinks it's a great idea, but Esteban isn't so sure. "What does she know?" he asks with a scowl.

But Elena believes in Naomi, and to prove it, she puts her in charge of the dig.

"I promise to do a great job!" Naomi says.

The next day, Elena, Naomi, Esteban, and Professor Mendoza begin the dig. But before long, Esteban tells Naomi she's doing it all wrong.

"I'll show you," he says, taking her pick. He swings it at the wall and makes a huge hole! **CRACK!** The entire wall comes crashing down!

Suddenly, an elf-like creature leaps out at them with a giggle!
"POKA-POKA-BABALOO!" the strange creature says.

"What is that?" cries Naomi.

"A *duende*!" Professor Mendoza exclaims. "*Duendes* are mischievous elves from a magical world."

"Legend says that three *duende* brothers came to Avalor many years ago, playing tricks on people and even stealing things," the professor explains. "But a wizard caught them and locked them in three separate ruins."

"My atlas can show us where the other *duende* brothers are," says the professor. But as soon as the *duende* sees the book, he swipes it out of her hands and runs!

"You were in charge," Esteban tells Naomi. "And now a *duende* is on the loose."

"Don't worry!" Naomi says with determination. "I'll catch him!"

With Naomi leading the way, they finally catch up to the *duende*. He's trying to open the door of an ancient pyramid.

But before they can form a plan, Esteban runs toward the creature, shouting, "Get away from there!"

The *duende* just smirks and then jumps up and gives Esteban's nose a pinch!

While Esteban howls in pain, the *duende* forces open the pyramid door. There's a gust of wind and out jumps a second *duende*! The brothers do a little victory dance and then run away.

"Look!" says Naomi, pointing to a drawing on the pyramid.

"It's a warning," Professor Mendoza says. "Each *duende* wears a necklace with a magic gem. Together, the three gems form a key that can unlock a magical tunnel. Then thousands of mischievous *duendes* could enter Avalor."

"But they haven't freed the third *duende* yet," Elena says. "Let's go!"

The four of them hop in a boat and head for the third ruin. They arrive before the *duendes*, so Naomi grabs a net from the boat to build a trap.

As soon as the brothers get there, Esteban releases the trap. "We got you!"

But the *duendes* outsmart him, flinging the net over Elena, Naomi, Esteban, and Professor Mendoza instead! Then they release the third brother.

Esteban lurches toward the *duendes* but trips,
pulling everyone down into the ruin with him.

"AAAAAHHHHHHH!"

They land at the bottom in a heap.

"This is what we get for putting Naomi in charge," Esteban growls as he struggles to his feet.

Naomi feels terrible. "Maybe Esteban was right about me all along."

"You're smart, brave, and resourceful," Elena says. "We need you."

Naomi smiles up at her friend. Then she gets an idea.

"We can use the net as a ladder!"

As the group climbs up out of the ruin, they're met by the jaquins. Migs tells Elena about some weird little elves at the port stealing ropes and cargo hooks.

"Why would they steal that stuff?" Elena wonders.

"Only one ruin is so high that you need climbing gear," Professor Mendoza says. "The Suncliff!"

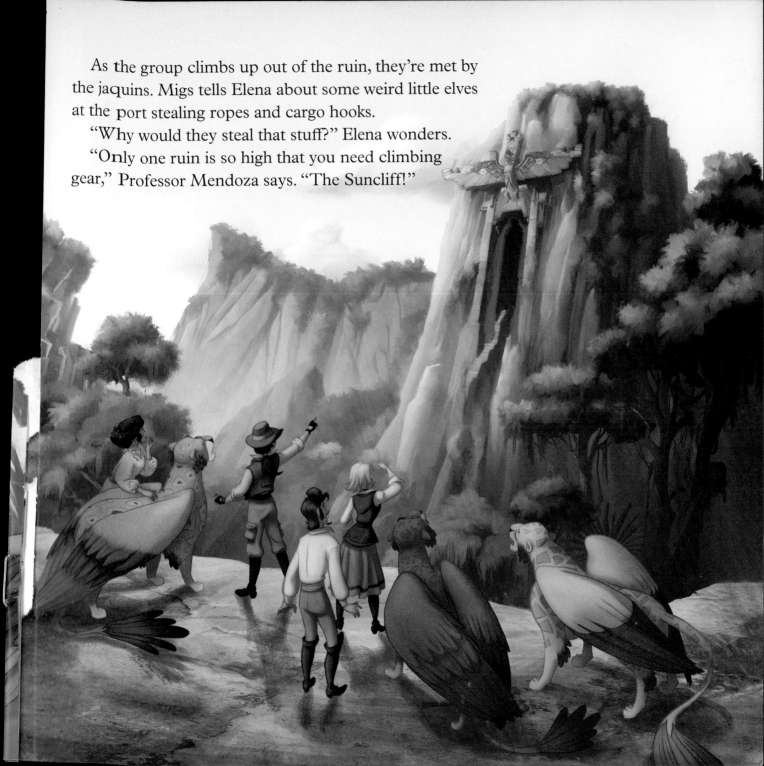

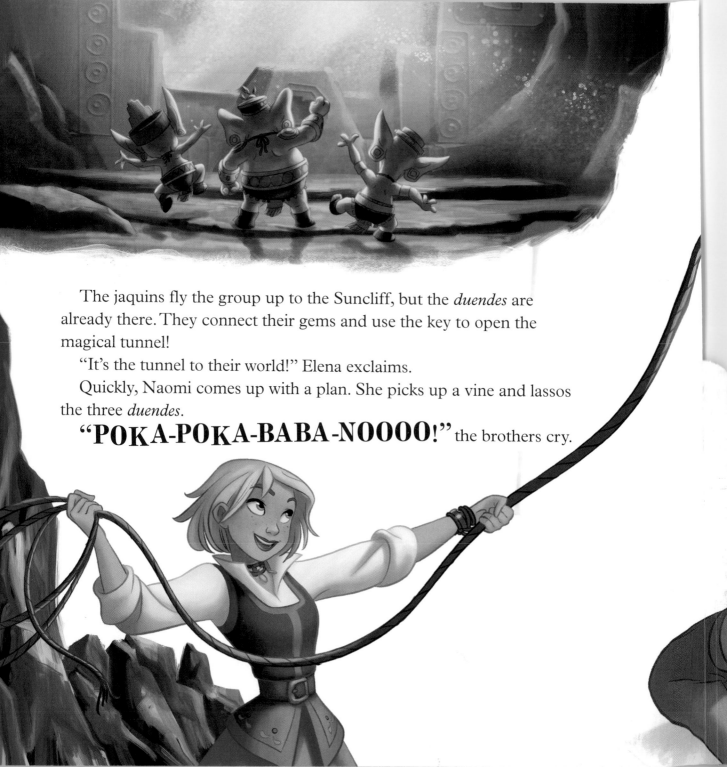

The jaquins fly the group up to the Suncliff, but the *duendes* are already there. They connect their gems and use the key to open the magical tunnel!

"It's the tunnel to their world!" Elena exclaims.

Quickly, Naomi comes up with a plan. She picks up a vine and lassos the three *duendes*.

"POKA-POKA-BABA-NOOOO!" the brothers cry.

As the group climbs up out of the ruin, they're met by the jaquins. Migs tells Elena about some weird little elves at the port stealing ropes and cargo hooks.

"Why would they steal that stuff?" Elena wonders.

"Only one ruin is so high that you need climbing gear," Professor Mendoza says. "The Suncliff!"

The jaquins fly the group up to the Suncliff, but the *duendes* are already there. They connect their gems and use the key to open the magical tunnel!

"It's the tunnel to their world!" Elena exclaims.

Quickly, Naomi comes up with a plan. She picks up a vine and lassos the three *duendes*.

"POKA-POKA-BABA-NOOOO!" the brothers cry.

With a strong tug, Naomi flings them into the tunnel. Then Elena, the professor, and Esteban remove the key to close it back up. The *duendes* are sealed in their world once more.

"We did it!" shouts Naomi.

Back at the palace, Elena tells her grandparents how the kingdom was saved thanks to Naomi.

"It's a good thing Naomi was in charge," Elena says. "Right, Esteban?"

Esteban shrugs. "I am sorry for not believing in you, Naomi."

"Thanks!" Naomi says with a grin. "Now who's ready to finish the dig?"